Hello, Family Members,

Learning to read is one of the most important accomplishments of early childhood. **Hello Reader!** books are designed to help children become skilled readers who like to read. Beginning readers learn to read by remembering frequently used words like "the," "is," and "and"; by using phonics skills to decode new words; and by interpreting picture and text clues. These books provide both the stories children enjoy and the structure they need to read fluently and independently. Here are suggestions for helping your child *before*, *during*, and *after* reading:

Before

• Look at the cover and pictures and have your child predict what the story is about.
• Read the story to your child.
• Encourage your child to chime in with familiar words and phrases.
• Echo read with your child by reading a line first and having your child read it after you do.

During

• Have your child think about a word he or she does not recognize right away. Provide hints such as "Let's see if we know the sounds" and "Have we read other words like this one?"
• Encourage your child to use phonics skills to sound out new words.
• Provide the word for your child when more assistance is needed so that he or she does not struggle and the experience of reading with you is a positive one.
• Encourage your child to have fun by reading with a lot of expression . . . like an actor!

After

• Have your child keep lists of interesting and favorite words.
• Encourage your child to read the books over and over again. Have him or her read to brothers, sisters, grandparents, and even teddy bears. Repeated readings develop confidence in young readers.
• Talk about the stories. Ask and answer questions. Share ideas about the funniest and most interesting characters and events in the stories.

I do hope that you and your child enjoy this book.

—Francie Alexander
   Chief Education Officer,
   Scholastic's Learning Ventures

To Justin, a little boy
I am very thankful for
—M.P.

Go to www.scholastic.com for web site information on
Scholastic authors and illustrators.

ISBN 0-439-32101-8

Library of Congress Cataloging-in-Publication Data

Packard, Mary
     It's Thanksgiving Day! / by Mary Packard; illustrated by Carolyn Ewing
and Sylvia Walker
     p. cm. – (Hello reader! Level 1)
     "Cartwheel books."
     Summary: Thanksgiving Day is a busy day as a boy tries to help his family prepare
for the arrival of relatives and the serving of a lovely meal.
     ISBN 0-439-32101-8 (pbk.)
     [1. Thanksgiving Day—Fiction. 2. Stories in rhyme.] I. Ewing, C.S., ill. II. Title. III.
Series.
     PZ8.3.P125 Iv 2001
[E]—dc21   2001020759

10 9 8 7 6 5 4 3 2   01 02 03 04 05
Printed in the U.S.A.
First printing, October 2001

It's Thanksgiving Day!

by Mary Packard
Illustrated by Carolyn Ewing
and Sylvia Walker

Hello Reader! — Level 1

SCHOLASTIC INC.

New York   Toronto   London   Auckland   Sydney
Mexico City   New Delhi   Hong Kong

The turkey is in the oven.
Grandma has come to stay.
The house smells oh so yummy.
It's Thanksgiving Day today.

Mom and Dad are busy.
There's so much to be done.
It sure is good that I'm around.
I'm helping everyone.

Grandma is in the kitchen.
She's very busy, too.

When she isn't looking,
I sneak a taste or two.

I help Dad make the table
as long as it can be.
We use four leaves to make it big
for all our company.

I help set the table
with lots of pretty things.
Susie fits the napkins
inside the napkin rings.

Mom cooks sweet potatoes.
I like them very much.

The marshmallows I put on top
are just the perfect touch.

Daddy makes fresh cider
with our apple press.

Susie thinks she's helping—
but she's making a big mess.

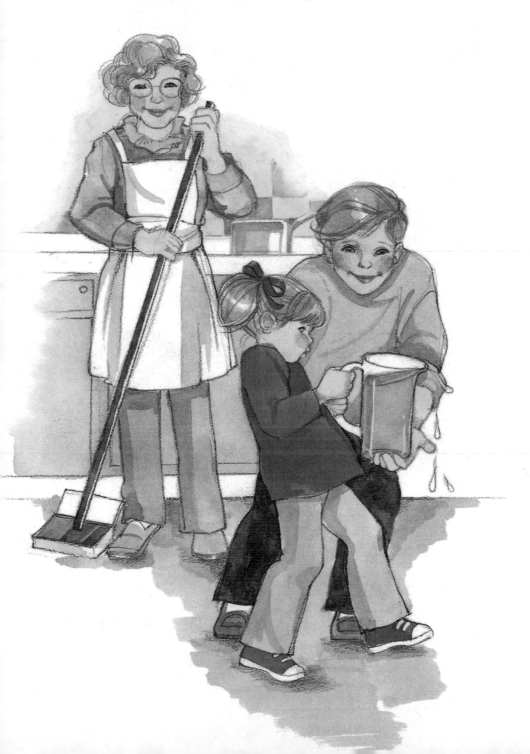

I hear the doorbell ringing.
The company is here.
Aunt Betty brings her pumpkin pies.
She bakes them every year.

We sit down at the table
in a happy mood.
We tell why we are thankful
before we eat the food.

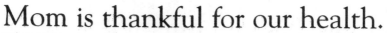
Mom is thankful for our health.

Aunt Jane had a good year.

I am glad my cousins came.

Grandma's thankful we're all here.

Dad is thankful nothing's burned.
He is such a tease!

And Susie's really thankful
that we're not having peas.

We eat the food that looks so good now that we've had our say.

And we hope that next
Thanksgiving . . .

will be just like today!